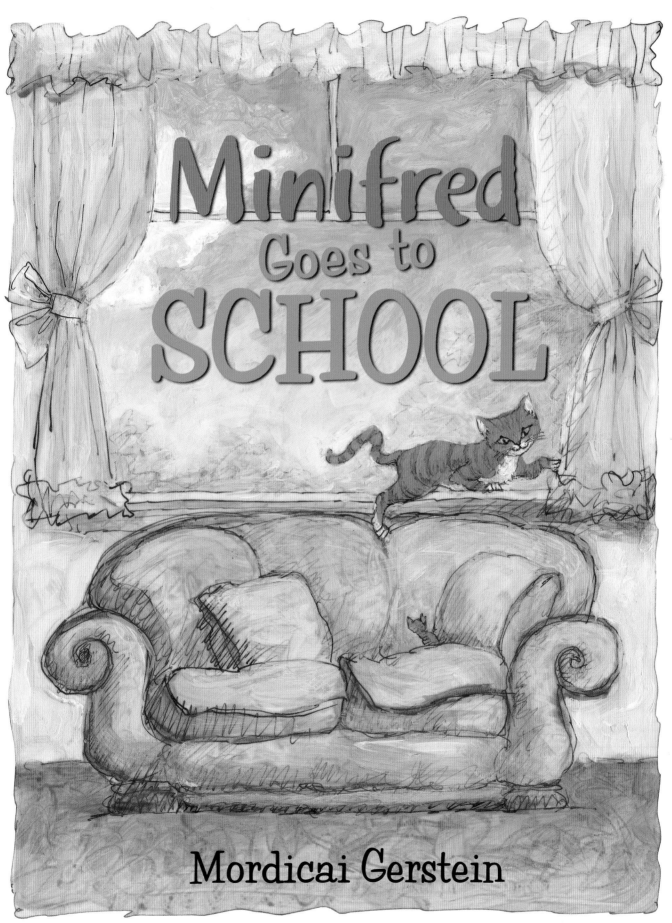

Minifred Goes to SCHOOL

Mordicai Gerstein

HarperCollinsPublishers

Library of Congress Cataloging-in-Publication Data
Gerstein, Mordicai.
Minifred goes to school / by Mordicai Gerstein. — 1st ed.   p.   cm.
Summary: When Mr. Portly finds a kitten, he and his wife raise her like a child, but unlike a typical child, Minifred the kitten does not like to follow rules at home or at school.
ISBN 978-0-06-075889-9 (trade bdg.) — ISBN 978-0-06-075890-5 (lib.)
[1. Cats—Fiction. 2. Animals—Infancy—Fiction. 3. Obedience—Fiction. 4. School—Fiction.] I. Title.
PZ7.G325Mi 2009   2008013861   [E]—dc22   CIP   AC

Typography by Rachel Zegar   1 2 3 4 5 6 7 8 9 10   ❖   First Edition

This book is for Susan. With all my love.

"Lavonne!" Mr. Portly called to his wife.
"Guess what I found while vacuuming under the sofa
cushions. Hint: It's something we've been wanting."
"A baby?" guessed Mrs. Portly, running down the stairs.

"You're close," whispered Mr. Portly.
Cupped in his palms was a tiny kitten.
Its green eyes looked newly opened.

"Where did *you* come from?" they both asked.
"Mew mew!" it said.
The kitten was a girl and they named her Minifred,
after Mr. Portly's great-aunt, whom she resembled.

They fed Minifred warm milk from a doll's baby bottle.
She wore doll clothes saved from Mrs. Portly's childhood.
Her bed was a doll cradle.

Minifred grew quickly.
After two weeks the doll clothes no longer fit.
Mr. Portly brought home real baby clothes.

They fed her baby food with the spoon Mr. Portly's
mother used to feed him when he was a baby.
The Portlys treated Minifred just like a child, and
so she behaved like one. She did not like rules.

At five months, Minifred began walking on her hind legs.

One morning, when she was six months old,
she said "MAMA" instead of "mew mew."

She liked to sing
"Twinkle, Twinkle, Little Star."

She loved picture books . . .   and playing with string.

She chased mice and she ran
right up the walls after flies.
"That's against the rules!"
cried Mr. Portly.

"I don't approve of rules!" cried Minifred.
Some people thought she was a bit spoiled.

Her best friend, Olivia, lived next door.

They played hide-and-seek. Minifred never followed the rules.

When they had tea parties, Minifred liked to make a mess.

"What shall we play today?" Minifred asked one morning.

"It's no fun playing with you," said Olivia.
"You never follow the rules. Besides, I'm going to school."

"I want to go to school," Minifred told her parents, though she
wasn't really sure what school was.
"Why, of course!" they said, and off to school they went.

"We want to register our little girl," Mr. and Mrs. Portly said.

"Certainly," said the principal, looking carefully at Minifred,

"but are you *sure* she's a little girl?"

"She's obviously not a little boy," said Mr. Portly.

"Very well," said the principal.

"She will be in Mrs. Potchkey's class."

Mrs. Potchkey's class was fun.

When everyone sang, Minifred yowled.

Minifred learned the alphabet.

She enjoyed finger painting and used her toes too.
A fly flew past her nose.

She chased it up and down the wall.

"You are behaving like a kitten," said Mrs. Potchkey.

"Well, of course," said Minifred. "I am one."

"We obey rules," said Mrs. Potchkey.

"I don't obey anything,"
said Minifred,
"*especially*
not rules!"

"Then I
must send
you home," said
Mrs. Potchkey.
"You'll have to catch
me first!" cried Minifred.

Mrs. Potchkey and all the children
chased Minifred around the classroom . . .

down the hall . . .

through the girls' room . . .

through the boys' room . . .

through the nurse's office . . .

and into the principal's office . . .

. . . right into the principal's lap.
Minifred curled up and purred.

"This little girl," puffed Mrs. Potchkey, "is actually a kitten."
"I thought so," said the principal, rubbing Minifred's tummy.
"Are kittens allowed in school?" asked Mrs. Potchkey.

The principal looked in **The Big Rule Book**.

"I find no rule against it. But it says, 'ALL students must obey **all** the rules.'"

"May I go back to class now?" Minifred asked.

"Only if you obey the rules."

"I obey *nothing*!" cried Minifred. She jumped onto the principal's head and out the window.

Minifred grabbed the tail of a
kite and flew up over the school.
"Careful," called a sparrow.
"Don't go too high!"
"Mind your own business!" said Minifred,
and she flew higher.
"Come back!" cried Olivia.
"Minifred's parents must come to school,"
said the principal.

Minifred landed on the school weather vane.

She spun round and round.

"Whee!" said Minifred.

After a while her tummy felt a bit odd.

"Maybe," she thought, "it's time to go down."

Just then a car screeched to a stop in the street below.
Minifred saw her parents get out.

"Mommy! Daddy! Look!" she called, balancing on one toe.
But her parents couldn't hear her. They ran into the school.

Mr. and Mrs. Portly rushed into the office.
"What's the matter?" they asked. "Is Minifred hurt?
Does she have a fever? Is she hungry? Is she sad?"

"Mr. and Mrs. Portly," said the principal,
"are you aware that your daughter is a kitten?"

Minifred jumped through the window onto the principal's desk.
"Mommy, Daddy!" she cried. "The principal is being horrible!
She won't let me have any fun!"

"Minifred," said the principal, "will not obey any rules."
"Tell us something we don't know," said Mrs. Portly.

"And just where," asked Mr. Portly, "are these rules written?"
"In **The Big Rule Book**, of course," said the principal.

Rule 1:

ALL
students must
obey **all**
the rules.*

*Except kittens, who must do exactly as they like!

"Wait!" said Minifred. "What's the teensy writing under that?"

The principal looked through her magnifying glass.
"It says, 'Except kittens, who must do exactly as they like!'"

"Aha!" said Minifred. "That's the one rule I *always* follow."

"She does!" agreed the Portlys. "Every day!"

"May I go back to class now?" purred Minifred.

"Why . . . I . . . I . . ." stuttered the principal. "I guess so!"

And so Minifred Portly became an excellent
student at Watson Elementary.

She read fat books   and chased fat squirrels.

She ran up the walls.   She skidded down the halls.

"I always follow the rules!" she said proudly.

"It's not fair!" complained the other students.

"Why can't we do what Minifred does?"

"I think you know the answer," said Mrs. Potchkey.

"Because we're not kittens?" answered Olivia.

"That's *right!*" said Minifred.

Then she jumped out the window after a butterfly.